The Automagic Horse

**EXPLORE
NEW
WORLDS
—READ!**

This book has been donated by:

The Automagic Horse

By
L. Ron Hubbard

Illustrated by
Scott E. Sutton

Bridge
Publications, Inc.

THE AUTOMAGIC HORSE

For information, address Bridge Publications, Inc., 4751 Fountain Ave., Los Angeles, CA 90029

Cover Illustration by Scott E. Sutton

First Edition

10 9 8 7 6 5 4 3 2 1

ISBN 0-88404-906-X

Table of Contents

Reader's Note

In reading this book, be very certain you never go past a word you do not fully understand.

The only reason a person gives up a study or becomes confused or unable to learn is because he or she has gone past a word that was not understood.

The confusion or inability to grasp or learn comes AFTER a word that the person did not have defined and understood.

Have you ever had the experience of coming to the end of a page and realizing you didn't know what you had read? Well, somewhere earlier on that page you went past a word that you had no definition for or an incorrect definition for.

Here's an example: "It was found that when the crepuscule arrived the children were quieter and when it was not present, they were much livelier." You see what happens. You think you don't understand the whole idea, but the inability to understand

ZZZZZ

came entirely from the one word you could not define, *crepuscule*, which means twilight or darkness.

It may not only be the new and unusual words that you will have to look up. Some commonly used words can often be misdefined and so cause confusion.

As an aid to the reader, words most likely to be misunderstood have been defined in the glossary included at the back of this book. The words in the book which are defined in the glossary are marked with an * the first time they appear. Words often have several meanings. The definitions used in this glossary only give the meaning that the word has as it is used in the book. This glossary is not meant as a substitute for a dictionary. Be sure to use a dictionary when you read. It makes it easy to learn and enjoy new things.

Introduction

Although *The Automagic Horse* is set in the Hollywood of the 1940s—nearly fifty years ago—it is really not all that different from the Hollywood of today. The hero is one of those "crazy" creative types, always battling the studio money men. His interest is making dreams a reality; theirs is making profits a reality.

Gadget O'Dowd is our character's name, and his job is to create special effects for movies. If you wanted a monster who shot flames from his mouth every time he opened it, you would call Gadget, for he was a genius at his work. In this case, Gadget has to build the most lifelike mechanical horse ever seen. But even though he loves the challenge, Gadget has something more important on his mind—a secret project. The problem is, he needs money for his dream project and . . .

You have to read the book to discover how Gadget gets into trouble, and if he manages to get out of it.

L. Ron Hubbard knew the Hollywood he writes about very well. He first worked there in 1937. Already well known to readers across the country for his adventure, western, romance, flying sports, detective and other stories, he was asked to come to Hollywood by Columbia Pictures. The studio wanted to use his name to launch what they called a Super Serial, a big-budget, big-name continuing weekly adventure, shown in movie theaters around the country. So it came about that he was offered what in those days was a large amount of money to come to Hollywood and write fifteen film scripts. The serial was to be based upon his novel *Murder at Pirate Castle*—and would be renamed *Secret of Treasure Island.*

Ron lived again in Hollywood in 1947 and 1948—the time during which *The Automagic Horse* was written. And the friends he made included many actors, directors and others who worked in different parts of the movie business.

It was a business he learned to love. And one which he continued to have interest in throughout his life. In fact, he even directed instructional films and wrote many more scripts in his later years.

His love for film and liking for the people involved in it is very apparent in *The Automagic Horse.* His colorful characters and realistic descriptions of filmmaking leap off the pages to fully capture the magic of the movies. And this is given even further life by talented California artist Scott E. Sutton, who has illustrated children's books since 1986.

But L. Ron Hubbard's trademark as a writer has always been excitement and suspense, and there's plenty of that here too. So, Lights! Camera! Action! Saddle up for *The Automagic Horse* and enjoy the ride!

Gadget Gets a New Job

"It ain't the principle of the thing, it's the money," said Gadget O'Dowd. "The day when I can build you a reasonable model of a racehorse like Man-of-War* for ten thousand dollars, I'll know recession is here!"

Mike Doyle, the assistant chief of the Technical Division of the Property Department of United Pictures, slumped sadly behind his desk, looking at Gadget. Ordinarily they were friends but they had reached a deadlock.*

"Gadget," said Mike, "we pay you two thousand dollars a week to be a construction genius. Look at what you've done in the past. And now you're trying to balk* at a lousy little old mechanical horse."

Gadget was slender, redheaded, snub-nosed and Irish. He was trying to look frank just now but for all that he could not quite hide a single fact about himself—he was a man who harbored* an enormous secret.

He had been christened George Carlton O'Dowd and he had enough university degrees to comfortably paper a large office. He could have been the chief of any number of vast research organizations but instead he was an effect specialist for United Pictures. The reason was top-secret. And it demanded money.

"This budgeteering* will ruin me yet," said Gadget. "It is getting so a man can't make a dishonest dollar unless he's first cousin to the president of this company. I can't make a horse that will do what you want unless you up that budget. And that's final!"

Mike Doyle got up and sat down again on the edge of his desk. He was earnest and persuasive. "Now listen, Gadget, have a heart. I can't help what these management men are trying to do. They give me my duties and tell me what I am supposed to do. And that's that. Look at the spot we are in. The script says here"—and he tapped it—"that Miss Morris has to gallop a horse out of the middle of a burning barn, bust through the doors and escape from Peter Butler who's got the place ringed with his gunmen.

"Now, Gadget, you know doggone well that the Society for the Prevention of Cruelty to Animals ain't going to let us use no live horse. This scene has gotta be big, with lots of flame, and the roof caves in immediately after the stunt man gets out of there. Now if he didn't get a chance to batter the doors down and the roof fell in and it was a live horse we was using, the S.P.C.A. would be down on us like a ton of bricks.* You just plain got to give us a decent horse. You know what happened to *Diana and the Devil?*"

"No," said Gadget, disinterestedly, "what?"

"Well, that little dog they used in there that was supposed to rescue the kid out of the duck pond up and got pneumonia and died. The S.P.C.A. got Ladies Aid Societies all over the country to ban that picture. It must have cost us a million and a half. Gadget, you just got to get us that horse!"

"If the money boys upstairs want to give a dog pneumonia and lose a million and a half, that's their problem," said Gadget. "I've got to think about my expenses."

"And you got to think about your old age," said Mike. "I'll tell you what I'll do. I'm a friend of yours. I'll call up McDonnell and see if he won't stretch that budget to fifteen thousand."

Gadget waited while Mike had his secretary put through the call. McDonnell was in the studio barbershop and it took two or three minutes to reach him. Gadget fidgeted while Mike talked.

"But you know how it is," Mike was saying. "I tell you, Mr. McDonnell, even horse meat has gone up. The special-effects man is in here now and he tells me that it can't be done for a cent less than twenty thousand bucks." There were long silences broken by grunts from Mike. He occasionally winked at Gadget. "All right," said Mike. "If that's all you'll do, that's all you'll do. I know you got people on your neck, too. All right, Mr. McDonnell. Yes, that's the movie business. Goodbye, sir." Mike hung up and turned to Gadget.

"I got it up to eighteen thousand dollars. If you can't do it for that, we'll have to use stunt men in a horse skin."

Gadget was all lightness and cheer now. He had expected fifteen thousand dollars as a top figure. His head was already working with plans of what he would do to that horse. He patted Mike affectionately on the shoulder and went out. He gave the secretaries a

few wicked winks as he passed them, and he started whistling the moment he was out in the sunshine.

Hands deep in his pockets, Gadget sauntered* on down toward the gate. He was just veering off course to pick a carnation from the Stage* Six garden for *The Buccaneer* when he heard his name excitedly called behind him.

He turned to find himself pursued by Mike. He sadly shut his mental calculator.

"Just a minute, Gadget," said Mike, out of breath. "McDonnell must have got kicked around in the business office. He called back to say that he'd have to put an accountant on the job with you."

"An accountant!" gaped Gadget, his snub nose getting aggressive.

"I can't help it," said Mike. "Things are getting tough all over."

Gadget finally shrugged, "Well, that's the movie business. So long, Mike." And he wandered toward the gate, the carnation forgotten, gloom overcasting the sun.

Tony Marconio, his gardener-butler-chauffeur, a weasel-faced little man who played gangster parts whenever Central Casting could find him in its enormous files, popped out to open the door for him.

"What'sa matter, Gadget?" said Tony.

"We have an accountant coming up to hold a club over our heads," gloomed Gadget. " 'Don't use so much ink.' 'You've used up your share of screwdrivers for Tuesday,' " mimicked Gadget. " 'I'm sure two drops and not three drops of machine oil would do just as well.' Blah! The movie business!"

"Things could be woise,"* said Tony, popping in back of the wheel and sending the open limousine out through the gate like a lightning bolt. "I picked up a few bucks on Roamin' Baby in the fifth race at Santa Anita."*

"Don't mention horses to me," said Gadget, and he sank down to glare at the sides of Cahuenga Pass as they ripped by.

Gadget's Top-Secret Plan

The studio would not permit Gadget to have his laboratory on the lot since it had twice blown up, menacing, they scolded him, "the lives and properties of United Pictures," to say nothing of the last blast's having knocked the wig from a producer's head at an extremely unfavorable moment.

They had bought him a slice of land in Sherman Oaks on the theory that the people who lived around there didn't matter and that a range of hills between their special-effects man's dabbling and the property of United Pictures was a fine thing to have.

The open limousine sliced on up Ventura Boulevard past Repulsive Pictures at Laurel Canyon and careened* into the exclusive side road which led to Gadget's personal property. When they screeched to a halt at the door, old Angus McBane, complete with blacksmith's apron, tobacco-stained handlebar mustache and a tam-o'-shanter,* was on hand to hear the news.

McBane and Tony Marconio made up Gadget's "family." Angus was a Scotch master mechanic who had been reeducated, much against his will, by engineer Gadget O'Dowd. In return he had done considerable educating of his own. Angus could make anything from a lady's wrist watch to an atom bomb, providing Gadget gave him the general details.

"I suppose ye've failed," said Angus.

"Nope," said Gadget, getting out and looking thoughtfully at his laboratory. "They upped it to eighteen thousand."

"Aye?" said Angus, hastily hiding his surprise. "But I suppose there was many a string attached to it?"

"There was," said Gadget. "We have to take on an accountant."

"An accountant!" cried Angus. "Ye mean I'll have to account for every measly* wee bit of tin, and cut the corners, and save string?"

"I'm afraid so," said Gadget.

"It isna* worth it, laddie. Where and away noo will we be getting the new wing for the shop?"

The three of them looked at the low rambling* structure. It was painted white and had window boxes. It appeared to be as innocent as any rose-covered cottage. But this laboratory ran back into the Hollywood Hills for a good eighth of a mile. Its chambers and rooms were equipped with all manner of scientific bric-a-brac.* The projected* left wing was a long spur* which would go underground far enough to permit an experimentation with gamma rays.* It costs money to drill solid rock, particularly when it has to be reinforced against possible earthquakes. They had counted on this present job to complete the construction.

"Let's all go in and have a drink," said Gadget. And they sadly filed into the main room which was a combination bar, museum and lounge. Tony mixed up three buttermilk shakes, since the alcohol on the shelves behind was strictly for visitors, by common consent.

"I know he tried," said Tony.

"Well, I didna* expect any more," said Angus, wiping the buttermilk from his handlebar mustache. "Noo, Chief, what burdensome task begins this sad travail?"*

"Well, it's got to be a horse," said Gadget. Something like inspiration came into his eyes. His stature grew. His red hair glowed. "It's got to be a horse that will run and buck and break down a door and be fairly fireproof. I think maybe you'd better start in with a hide."

He was thinking now. Like an artist who begins to conceive a great masterpiece, he forgot the financial worry and his own current project in the joy of pure creation. "I'll take care of the skeletal structure as soon as I can get to the drawing board.

There's a picture of a horse skeleton around here someplace. I'll use that new battery motor we built for *Frankenstein's Mate*. But the thing is, it has got to look real. It has got to act real. It's got to be a masterpiece! Angus, first thing you do is find a hide. I'll fireproof it; you just find a hide."

"Who's going to fireproof the stunt man?" said Tony.

"There isn't any S.P.C.A. for stunt men," reproved Gadget. "Now, Angus, you get out and find me a horse."

"We canna kill it," said Angus. "There's no difference between murderin' one and burning another."

"Well now, don't bother me with petty details," said Gadget. "I'm thinking. You just get out and find me a good horse hide—head, ears, everything. We can use that blind-man radar from *The Bat's Return* for his eyes. Now let me see . . ."

Angus hung up his leather apron behind the bar, removed his tam-o'-shanter and got into an old tweed coat. "How much'll I pay, laddie?"

"Steal it if possible. When that accountant gets here we'll tell him—"

A cool voice behind them said, "You'll tell her what?"

They whirled to find themselves looking at a girl who could have been a stand-in for a famous movie star. She was beautifully dressed, with stylish hair. She had everything about her to add charm and femininity which Hollywood could devise. But for all that there was a grim precision which came from something unseen. It made her, as Gadget estimated in the first glance, about as lovable as one of his special effects for *The Ghost Rider*.

"I am Miss Franklin, from the business office," she said, extending her hand.

Gadget took it as though he expected it to carry thirty or forty thousand volts.* "That was just a joke," he said weakly.

"I'm sure it was," said Miss Franklin. "At least I hope so. I have been looking over your budget and various expenses, Mr. O'Dowd. The office has warned me to be very careful."

"Have some buttermilk," said Gadget hastily.

"Dishonesty," she announced, "is a thing I cannot tolerate."

"Miss," said Angus, bristling, "this lad dinna* have a crooked hair on his head."

"Well," said Miss Franklin, "I shouldn't think it would be necessary for a man who already draws* a salary of two thousand dollars a week."

"Miss," began Angus, ends of his mustache sticking straight up, "I—"

Whatever it was he would have said was drowned in a clank and roar from the far side of the room. Tony, behind the bar, had pressed a remote control button and now the Moloch monster, used in *The Lost Tribe*, with a yard of flame shooting out of his face, stepped away from the wall with a sound like scrunching bones. He reached out his arms toward Miss Franklin.

Any normal human girl, as they had many times in the past, would have fainted then and there. But not Miss Franklin. She cuffed* Moloch soundly on the jaw and sat him down with a dreadful clatter of jarred parts.

"That was very effective on the screen," said Miss Franklin, "but I think it rather childish of you to keep it around. May I ask where my office is?"

Struck dumb, Gadget escorted her through a door into an office which he usually turned over to visiting engineers. He left her to spread out her account books and pencils on the desk. He noted that she did it in a disgustingly precise manner. Now he would *never* make any progress with that gamma room tunnel.

In his own office, Gadget stared out the window. He did not even notice when Tony removed his coat and slid him into his turquoise working jacket. He sank down at his drawing board and picked up his pencil.

"Well, there's other jobs," said Tony.

"Not that pay two thousand a week," said Gadget.

"Well, you don't have to keep on wit' the project," said Tony.

Gadget looked at him, suddenly stricken. Tony recoiled, realizing his mistake.

"I'm sorry!" said Tony. "I know what we got to do. I was just kiddin', Chief."

Gadget shot out another glare and looked back at the board. Tony said no more about it. It was, in fact, entirely against the law to mention it around here. But all this slaving and sweating and dollar grubbing* was on the highroad* to as gallant* and daring a project as mankind could imagine. The three of them were dedicated, soul and pocketbook, to an endeavor which would have made even the great movie producer Samuel Goldwyn dizzy.

They weren't going to make a supercolossal movie epic. They weren't going to overthrow United Pictures. They weren't going to elect a president. No, their dreams had no such finite limits.

Gadget and Company were headed for the moon!

And after that Mars!

And after that stars!

Real stars. Not movie stars.

Lying in the winding passages of this workshop, woven into every plan, staring out of each

scheme, was the nose of the *Voyageur I*, a spaceship destined to make history!

No minor research job for Gadget like chief of Westinghouse* Laboratory; no little niche* like head of the army or navy; no peanut-sized job like the presidency of the United States or the boss of the United Nations.* This Irishman had slightly larger plans. He intended to make a test voyage around the moon and then a full jaunt* to Mars. Following which he was going to break the "wall of light"* and get out there where they had some man-sized planets.

Who would trade the earth and any job on it for the full possession of some king-sized satellites around some giant-class stars? Not Gadget. He was going to give Earth an empire that *was* an empire and become immortal in the bargain.

Every penny he could beg, cheat for or even earn was tied up in the *Voyageur I*. Every one of his experiments was slanted to some improvement of that ship. Actual parts of it were scattered here and there through these laboratories and its full design, constantly modified, was guarded by a safe in the floor so burglarproof that the FBI in full force couldn't have cracked it.

This was the secret of Gadget O'Dowd and this was the plan to which his "family" was dedicated to the death. Top-secret. Top!

Tony tiptoed out of there, knowing better than to say another word. He listened at the door and after a while heard Gadget's fountain pen scratching away at the horse drawings. Tony moved away.

Peeking into Miss Franklin's office he saw her sitting, making entries in her account books. He made a face at her back and went out to prune the orange trees. They were very special orange trees, mineralized artificially so as to produce super orange juice which, some day, would be condensed and canned for the supplies of a space-ship to prevent, at one drop per day, any possible quantity of space scurvy.[*]

A chipmunk chattered at him. Tony suddenly drew a gun from an equally imaginary shoulder holster and fired six death-dealing shots at the chipmunk.

"Take dat! And dat, you stinking swine!"[*] said Tony. "I'll massacre— Don't shoot! Don't shoot!" But he was shot and he staggered to his knees to do a fine death scene he had witnessed in a Humphrey Bogart[*] movie last night. Much cheered then, he got up, recovered his shears and clipped away at the twigs. He began to whistle an opera introduction.

Miss Franklin Takes Charge

The following afternoon an incident occurred which sounded the general alarm loud enough to call both Gadget and Tony from a hasty lunch. They rushed into the first chamber of the workshop where electrical effects were ordinarily made and were startled into immobility by a very strange sight.

Miss Franklin, who, as far as Gadget could find out, had no first name, was there. She was dressed in a lovely afternoon gown with a pair of horn-rimmed glasses perched on her very smudged nose. Her pencil was poised aggressively over a notebook. Facing her was Angus McBane, half covered by a horse hide which he had been in the act of dragging through the door. Angus saw with relief that reinforcements were approaching from the other entrance.

"Gadget, she's taking an inventory!" said Angus.

If he had told Gadget and Tony that Miss Franklin had been caught stealing from the cash box, they could not have been more shocked. Gadget glared.

"Miss Franklin, I think this is going a little too far. After all, you will find a complete inventory in my office. I am sure everything is on it which is the property of United Pictures. This distrust is heartbreaking. I cannot understand how you might suppose that we would have been so careless as to leave important objects off that inventory. Now, these rooms are no place for a lady. That equipment you are looking at was used to furnish the dead man's scene in *The Mad Doctor*. It is rigged to jump a hundred thousand volts between those electrodes.* Anyone coming in here is liable to get injured. Then how would I explain to the studio?

"I swear to you, Miss Franklin, that you will find our inventory—"

Her voice sawed into his speech like a sharpened icicle. "Mr. O'Dowd, I have already found twenty-five transformers,* seventeen condensers* and something which is labeled 'an alpha pile'* and nine cathode-ray tubes* which do not occur on that so-called inventory of yours. I suppose you can account for those satisfactorily?"

Gadget rallied.* "They are my own equipment which I have loaned free of charge to United Pictures. I have not said one word—"

"Mr. O'Dowd, you know very well that we have rules against private property in a studio technical laboratory. It must be registered with the studio. How else could one keep these matters straight? If you have been so slack in registering your own property and accounting for how you came by it, I cannot help but suppose that there are other irregularities. I am afraid that I must conduct an entire inventory of everything here."

Gadget looked as though he were on the verge* of fainting.

"And how aboot* my ain* tools?" said Angus. "I couldna work wi'out* them. And they are so numerous that t'would* take weeks just to list them."

"I suppose you want me to list my driving gloves, too," said Tony acidly. "See here, Boss. You want I should rub dis dame out?"*

Miss Franklin looked coolly at Gadget's man. "Corn,"* she said. "Pure corn. No wonder you aren't even a bit player* anymore. For your information, your driving gloves *should* be registered. According to paragraph three of section five of the accountancy regulations, everything which is used in the execution of studio business is either the property of the studio or must be registered with it for proper rental fees."

Gadget instantly brightened. "Well then, Miss Franklin, I fear we shall have to stop work on this horse long enough to carry out the inventory which you will require."

"On the contrary, Mr. O'Dowd, I do

not think that will be necessary. I have here a breakdown of past budgets. Checking back to the inventory I find that there are many items included in past budgets which do not appear on the inventory. I would suggest that you get on with your horse. I shall continue the business of protecting United's property. If there is any difference, you can take it up with me later."

Gadget leaned his head up against the door jamb and beat a futile* fist against the wall. "Give 'em control of money and you make czars* out of 'em. No wonder the Russians revolted." He faced her again and put out a pleading hand. "Miss Franklin, I am a scientist. You are an accountant. You are an expert in such matters, how could I help it if I made a few mistakes here and there? You—"

"A hundred and fifty thousand dollars is a lot of mistakes," said Miss Franklin. "But go on with your work. I am sure that after proper adjustment is made on these books, no word of it will reach the studio. But you have equipment here which should be sold and it is up to me to take care of that."

"Over my dead body," cried Angus. He threw down the horse hide. "Lady or no lady I—"

Gadget quickly stepped forward and slipped his arm through Miss Franklin's. "Let's go into the outer office," he said smoothly, "and talk this thing over quietly."

Miss Franklin wavered and then reached out her hand for the bill which Angus had been gripping. "I suppose that's the bill for the thing you are carrying?" said Miss Franklin.

Angus surrendered it. And Gadget was able to lead the pushy accountant into the main room. He was trying to distract her attention, but she read the bill anyway.

"My," she said, "that's a little bit high for a horse hide, twenty-eight hundred dollars. And he has even added taxi fare.

Gadget looked at it, wrinkling his brow. "Why, see here, he couldn't have a horse killed for the purpose. The only thing he could do was to get a stuffed horse out of the museum. That's natural now, isn't it? See? It says right here at the top, The Santa Ana Museum, stuffed relic of Stardust sired* by Man-of-War. You remember Stardust. She was a famous racer. Now you wouldn't expect to buy her for a measly twenty-eight hundred dollars, would you? She won a hundred and ninety thousand dollars in just one season. And," he added with some satisfaction, "after she goes through that fire, I'm afraid her hide won't be worth very much."

"Well—" said Miss Franklin, doubtfully, "I am not interested in the cost of individual items but only in the entire budget. I have no wish to obstruct your work, Mr. O'Dowd. I am afraid, however, that I shall have to pursue that inventory."

"Please," said Gadget, "let it go until a time when I can help you with it. Many of the items you will find are alive and dangerous. Why, just last week we had a truck driver executed by an electrical short circuit in a dinosaur from *Cave Man*." He got her back to his office and was shortly able to rejoin Angus.

Gadget picked up the horse hide.

"Why, it does look like Stardust," said Tony.

"Sure, and it is," said Angus. "Me and the curator was howlin' savage drunk half of the night. Somehow, in the scuffle, Stardust came oot* at the seams."

"What will happen to the bill?" said O'Dowd.

"Whin* the studio pays it, the curator will pay us back all but the ten percent that's to be his squeeze. After all, this is Hollywood."

"The movie business," said Tony with a sage* nod. He followed his two conspirators into the blacksmith's shop where Gadget had already sketched out on the wall the structural devices necessary for the skeleton. Angus resumed his apron and blew up the forge* so hot that his testing spit sizzled into steam a foot before it touched the fire. He picked up a bar of fine manganese* steel, glanced at the skeleton, and began to bend it.

" 'Tis a weary time that we'll have with that lassie," said Angus. "Twa* nights ago, when I saw the moon, 'twas through trees, and it boded* no good."

The place was soon a roaring, smoking mass of sparks and clangs. The automagic horse named Stardust was beginning to take form.

The Automagic Horse Comes to Life

During the following six weeks Gadget O'Dowd was so busy that he had little if any time to devote to his gravity repulsor.[*] The three test units of this machine and the parts of the main construction lay deep in a hidden and so far uninventoried part of the laboratory.

Miss Franklin was kept busy paying a stream of engineers and delivery boys from R.C.A.,[*] General Electric and Bell Telephone who brought odds and ends of electronic gear, looked happily at the steed, made suggestions and went on their way. Every tube,[*] booster[*] and transformer was carefully recorded in Miss Franklin's black book. Meanwhile, she went on about her inventory with a grim little smile. Now and then she triumphantly confronted the annoyed Gadget with some new item of his deceit.

"Now look here," Gadget said one morning when the horse was nearing completion, "you've just got to understand that you are a dame and you don't know what I need around here and what I don't."

"I have nothing to do with that," said Miss Franklin. "United Pictures doesn't care how much equipment you have so long as you are using it or intend to use it on their projects. Personally, it seems to me that you would be well off to get rid of a great deal of this material. It is terribly expensive and too duplicated* for any real use in the future. I think I shall recommend to the front office that we hold an electronic junk sale here."

"No, no," said Gadget, hastily. "When I get time I'll explain to you just why it is that we need every piece of this stuff."

"The explanation had better be good," said Miss Franklin.

"Oh, it is, it is," said Gadget. "But right now I have a horse to finish. Has that taxidermist* arrived yet?"

The taxidermist had. He was consoling himself at the bar where Tony had poured him a stiff drink. Gadget took the taxidermist and the drink back into the laboratory and showed him the completed skeletal structure.

"What an odd frame," said the taxidermist as he tapped it approvingly. "Limbs in proper proportion, face structure

perfect, and all in position and order. My word, Mr. O'Dowd, the National Museum could use you."

"That's what I'm afraid of," said Gadget.

The taxidermist was removing his maroon sport coat. "Stretching the hide over this shouldn't be too difficult, providing you haven't made it too large."

"Can you make skin flexible?" said Gadget. "That's the one problem that I haven't been able to lick."

"Oh, quite, certainly. I have some preservative oils here. But why should you want it flexible, Mr. O'Dowd?"

"Oh, just a whim of mine," said Gadget.

The taxidermist had picked up the skin and was again examining the skeletal structure when, for the first time, he saw the enormous maze of batteries, relays,* tubes, antennae and electrical bric-a-brac which filled in the horse's head and trunk.* It had been covered with paper to keep out the dust and he had thought that it was just stuffing. But when he pulled the paper away there was the amazing mass of wires and tubes. He backed up as fast as if Frankenstein's monster had just jumped him.

"My word!" he said. "Are you sure it isn't intended to explode?"

"Not a bit of it," said Gadget. "Now let's get down to the business of skin-stretching, what?"*

The taxidermist put on his saffron* working coat and went solemnly to work, restoring the head and hide of Stardust. Gadget puttered with some final adjustments in the interior.

"Now, cover up all those seams," said Gadget, "and make sure all those joints will move without cracking the skin."

"Move?" said the taxidermist.

"Move!" said Gadget.

"Well, my word," said the taxidermist. "This is the first time I've ever had this kind of a job. Well—that's the movie business."

"The movie business," agreed Gadget, nodding. Then he shoved his head deep into the maze of the stomach, busily setting the remote dials.

SCOTT E. SUTTON '94

Angus McBane came in from the forge room and put a hot metal bolt through the tail-moving mechanism, which completed his work. He stood back and took a big bite from a plug of Brown's Mule chewing tobacco and spat expertly clear across the room into the automatic-situating spittoon* they had had to build on a temporary loan of their services by United to Universal. The spittoon located the brown projectile by means of a radar beam and rolled noisily and hastily to get under it.

The taxidermist, catching this movement out of the corner of his eye, started back and gaped at the spittoon. He rubbed suspiciously at his glasses and then hesitantly went back to work.

Angus did it a second time and the spittoon clanged mightily to fulfill its mission. The taxidermist, this time, was alerted for it. He leaped as nervously as the spittoon.

"Whust* mon!" said Angus. "Hae ye never seen a trained spittoon? Back to ye're work, mon. Ye'll take care there with whut* ye're doin'. 'Tis a dangerous beastie ye're workin' upon. One loose seam or an onnatural*-fixed hair and he's like to explode with a most terrible bang!"

With this, Angus spat once more and went away to work happily upon some part of his spaceship.

Gadget finished up some of the remaining set adjustments on the control box and then, bored, wandered out to the outer office to see what Miss Franklin had been up to now. He found a brightly dressed and briefcased young man talking to the accountant. Introduction discovered him to be Mr. Jules Weinbaum, first cousin of

Artemis Weinbaum, producer of *Queens in Scarlet*, the picture for which the automagic horse was intended.

Naturally, Mr. Weinbaum had insurance to sell, and naturally Miss Franklin was buying it.

"Well, it's all cared for now," said Mr. Weinbaum. "I understand that you've almost completed the property, Mr. O'Dowd. I wish you a great deal of success with it." He shook hands again, ceremoniously, and went outside.

Miss Franklin filed the policy. "Now just because it's insured," she said, "don't get careless."

With some heat, Gadget retorted,* "You look after the dollars, Miss Franklin, and I'll look after the property."

"Well now," she said, "why be angry? I am

after all only trying to do my job, Mr. O'Dowd, and you will admit that your scientific absent-mindedness has caused a great deal of mix-up in these records. If I don't do my job, I'll lose it, and I need it. I need it very badly."

Gadget looked at her, feeling trapped and not knowing why. This accountant was not content to fight with all the weapons of her profession and the artillery of the business office, she was also using a woman's tears on him. Suddenly furious, he went into the bar and poured himself fully half a quart of buttermilk.

After two days of hard work the taxidermist was at the end of his task. He was a good taxidermist, but then, the technicians of Hollywood are very good indeed. It occasioned* no comment that the automagic horse was now Stardust indeed, in the flesh once more, unspotted by so much as a speck of museum dust. She was real down to the last hair. Stardust had a big white star on her forehead with flecks of white ranging back into the chestnut which sleekly covered the rest of her. She was indeed a very attractive horse.

Angus came in lugging a handsprayer and a bucket. They thoroughly doused her with invisible fireproofing.

"That's a good-looking filly," Gadget said to the taxidermist. "Thanks for a fine job." He went over to the control box and lifted it by its handle to a desk.

"What do you intend to do with it?" said the taxidermist. "I never mounted anything before that had to have its joints flexible."

Gadget was not paying any attention to him. He plugged in three relays, threw the switch and twisted a dial. Stardust instantly lifted up her head and let loose a shrill whinny, at the same time rearing* and pawing air. She faced around and showed the taxidermist both of her front hoofs. That good fellow did a back somersault, raced out the door, went past Miss Franklin and only paused long enough on the running board of his car to grab the check which she hastily brought to him. Then he was gone.

"What did you do to that man?" said Miss Franklin, thinking she heard Gadget at the door. But it was not Gadget, it was Stardust going through her first test, which was, of course, to batter down doors. The panel gave with a crash and the filly came through into the office, ducked under the front entrance and stood in the yard rearing and plunging.

Miss Franklin lay where she had fainted until O'Dowd found her and revived her. She looked fearfully at the splinters and then into the garden where stood a statue of a horse arrested* in mid-rear.*

"She does look kinda real at that," said Tony in appreciation. He and Gadget and Angus had, at this moment, become extremely fond of Stardust.

"Get me a horse trailer," said Gadget, grinning. "I've got to take her out to Santa Anita racetrack for a trial."

Miss Franklin made no protest and asked no questions. She promptly got up, went over to the telephone and dialed the San Fernando Trailers and ordered a horse trailer. She looked back at the horse as she laid down the phone. Then she looked at Gadget.

"It certainly looks real," she said. "I thought it was going to tear me to pieces."

"Well, she didn't," said Gadget, sadly.

Miss Franklin tidied up her hair and smoothed out her rumpled dress. "Well, that's the movie business," she said.

Gadget looked fondly at the horse. "Yes," he said, "that's the movie business."

Off to the Races!

Tony drove the Cadillac at a fast clip* towards Santa Anita. Gadget and Angus sat sadly in the rear seat. Behind them smoothly rolled a standard Hollywood horse trailer, satin-lined, painted a light blue to match the Cadillac, complete with a sun visor, drinking fountain, feed box and an automatic disposal unit. It was beginning to get dark as they drove down Colorado Street in Pasadena. They were almost there.

Gadget looked at his ruby-encrusted wrist watch. "I don't understand it," he said. "Everybody can rob the studios but us." And he broke the rule which he himself had made. "It isn't as if United wouldn't get the benefit of it. Why, when those headlines hit the papers United will be in about every fourth paragraph. They couldn't buy that publicity for ninety million bucks."

"And they would'na finance it for ten measly cents," said Angus.

"Maybe we can put some pressure on somebody," said Tony. "If kidnappin' just wasn't so illegal—"

"I don't wish Miss Franklin any hard luck," said Gadget, "but I wish she'd accidentally fall off the Colorado Street Bridge. It's going to cost us a couple of hundred thousand dollars to buy back our own equipment. And after all the trouble we had getting it, too."

"How much?" said Tony, shocked.

"Well, ninety thousand so far," said Gadget sadly.

"Maybe we could crack a bank,"* said Tony.

"Probably have to give up the whole expedition," said Angus.

Instantly he was fixed with glares from both Tony and O'Dowd. And he sank back with some self-satisfaction to gnaw* off his plug of Brown's Mule tobacco. He spat into the wind-stream and splattered the horse trailer with tobacco juice.

They wheeled into the gate and made themselves known to the guard. Gadget's studio card immediately gained them an attendant's services and dispersed the gathering dusk under an onslaught* of floodlights.

They stopped the car. The track wheeled away from them in both directions. The grandstands gaped emptily above them. A few grooms* and touts* were wandering around the stables in the far distance. Near at hand some losers still gloomed at the rail. Two other horse trailers were in sight. Gadget went beyond the starting gate so that his activities would be hidden from view.

Tony scrambled around and opened up the rear of the horse trailer. Gadget set up the control box under the rail. And Angus laid out a set of tools in case any adjustments had to be made. It was their intention to give Stardust a good thorough test. Otherwise, they could very well hold up production on *Queens in Scarlet* for a day or two by a minor breakdown, which item would cost the studio at least a hundred thousand dollars, due to stars' salaries, stage rentals and other expenses. One lost day's work just for the star, Veronica Morris, would be worth retiring on. Technicians have to be accurate in the movie business.

Tony set up two cases of soda and a package of sandwiches. Then he peeled off his chauffeur's coat to don* the frontier buckskin jacket which the stunt man would wear in the scene when he impersonated Veronica Morris. This was strictly for show. But, as Tony explained, "I gotta get into the mood for the part."

Stardust backed out of the trailer under her own power. She stood breathing quietly and occasionally snorting and flicking an ear, while Angus fixed the saddle on her. It was an English exercise pad* about half of the size of a postage stamp. Even so, little Tony's smallness made it seem quite large enough. Tony mounted and located the stirrups with his toes. He spoke encouragingly. Stardust moved her eyes, pawed and moved off with the sideways restlessness of a racehorse.

"Pretty good, huh?" said O'Dowd. "I spent two hours last night lookin' at some films of her when she was in her prime.* Now watch this."

Stardust shook her head in a huge negative, snorted and pranced[*] forward.

"Say, that's pretty good," said Tony. "I remember that. By golly, you got me half-tricked into believin' this *is* Stardust."

"Wul'[*] be keerful[*] of her, laddie," said Angus. "When she was alive she brought me nathing but trouble and sorrow. I remember losing seventy-five cents on her to that no-good bookie[*] Finklestein."

Stardust pranced and danced. Tony had to do a little expert riding to stay with her. But then, this was in Tony's line. In training up to be a bit player he had undertaken almost any sport you could name. He was fully as capable on a saddle as he was in an airplane. The only thing which kept him from being a stunt man was an irrational desire to go on living in one piece.

Gadget sent the horse down to the starting gate. Without any attention from the operator Stardust was able to find a box and go into it, stopping when she approached the gate itself.

"You are not going to run her?" said Angus.

"Well, according to the script," said Gadget, "she has to do a two-hundred-yard sprint after she gets out of that broken door. It's all in one shot, to convince the customers. So she'd *better* know how to run. All right there, Tony. Are you ready?"

"Let's go," said Tony. "Reminds me of Man-of-War. I wish this was a real race."

The floodlights glared down upon the track, the gate sprung and Stardust rushed forward, buck-jumping

the first six strides and then settling into a long, distance-devouring run. Tony, well into character now, laid on his whip and yelled encouragingly into the horse's ear. Gadget gestured at the control box and Angus took over. O'Dowd jumped up on top of the Cadillac, so he could see better.

Stardust went around the turn, came into the back stretch and began to thunder home. She was splitting the air like a lightning bolt.

Above the pound of hoofs Tony's shrill "Git! Git! Git!" and "Hi! Hi! Hi!" resounded.[*] Stardust came into the final stretch, speeded up and dashed across the finish line.

Gadget went down, took over the controls and brought the mount to a plunging halt. Stardust came trotting daintily back toward the parked trailer, tossing her head, jingling her bit and making snorty noises which indicated that she was out of wind.

"Boy, she sure can run," said Tony.

"We'll give her two more trials," said Gadget. "And then we'll go over to that old western town later tonight and batter down a couple of doors. She's got to be all ready by Wednesday."

He was about to turn a dial on the control box when he noticed three men standing at the rail, looking interestedly at the horse. He was about to ignore them when he recognized one of the men from his pictures. It was Cliff Neary, the comedian and racing dean,[*] who wasted the millions he made acting, on horses. Beside him was his trainer and an exercise boy.

"Just watching your horse run," said Cliff. "Didn't know that Stardust had any colts." Cliff put out his hand to Gadget. "I'm the owner of the Neary stables," he said. "This is my trainer, Hank."

"Gadget O'Dowd," said Gadget, shaking the extended hand.

"Oh yes," said Cliff. "The special-effects man. I remember that we contracted with United for some of your work on my *Road to Smolensk.*"

"*Road to Smolensk,*" said Gadget thoughtfully. "Oh yes, that was the vodka that broke into flame every time Roy Ellis spat."

"Good job," said Neary.

"There was nothing much to that. The things that were difficult in that picture didn't show at all."

"I know. You fellows never get much credit for all the little odds and ends that it takes to make a show happen. But what are you doing out here with a horse? I didn't know that was in your line."

"Well, she's kind of a funny horse," said Gadget.

"Mighty good-lookin' one," said the trainer, staring at Stardust hungrily.

"By the way," said Cliff, "you wouldn't like to race her against three or four of mine, would you?" He was trying not to look sly. "Nothing like a good horse race after a long, hard day's work at the studio."

Angus gaped and was on the verge of laughing when Gadget silenced him with a glare. "Well now," said Gadget trying not to appear eager but carelessly pulling half a dozen thousand-dollar bills out of his shirt pocket, "don't mind if I do."

"'Don't mind if I do' is right," said Cliff. "Hank, bring Thunder Mountain over here. Do you think you can push him through as a winner, Pat?"

Pat, a jockey, gave Cliff a white-toothed grin. "I reckon I can, Mr. Neary."

Tony watched all this with eyes which got wider and wider. Then he began to laugh. "Listen, pal," he said to the jockey, "this is pretty tough company you're riding in. The last three jocks that tried to beat me got buried, with horseshoes of roses. I don't beat easy, see?"

The jockey grinned and helped Hank bring Thunder Mountain up to the rail. The horse was a big, powerful stallion that Cliff had bought for quite a piece of change. He was being kept under blankets until the Neary Stables could make a large profit with him. Thunder Mountain, Cliff fondly believed, could make Man-of-War look like he was tied to a post.

Stardust breathed easily now and pranced a trifle, edging near Thunder Mountain. That steed, having horse sense, took one look at the fake filly and whistled shrilly, backing off.

"Whoa now, boy," said Cliff. "I never saw you lady-shy before."

Thunder Mountain reared, shook his head angrily, and whistled again, backing even further away from Stardust. Gadget took his cue* and removed his automagic horse down to the gate.

Gadget Gets Lucky

Presently they had both mounts behind the wire.* And the race was ready to be run. The trainer held up a blank cartridge pistol,* Angus got ready to release the gates, and Cliff eagerly yelled some final riding instructions to Pat. Gadget tried not to appear too interested in the control box on which he was sitting.

The gun roared. The gates sprang up. And horse and pseudo*-horse were off in a cloud of sawdust. Gadget had to trust to it that the last running speed would at least keep in distance of Thunder Mountain until they reached the home stretch. Then he hoped he could adjust matters. The six crisp thousand-dollar bills were weighted down by a rock, in company with another half dozen just like them which were fresh from Cliff's purse.

Angus, up higher, could see better. He began to make wild signals toward Gadget who turned up the running speed a notch.

The horse and pseudo-horse came into the back stretch with Thunder Mountain more than two hundred yards in the lead.

The shrill "Ki-yi" of Tony rose above the wheezes and grunts of the running mounts and the pounding of their hoofs. Angus was making despairing motions with his hands, and glancing sideways now and then at Gadget.

O'Dowd was not idle. He pulled up the dial and very noticeably Stardust began to close. When they were still seventy-five yards from the finish a wide gap yet remained. Gadget upped his dial another notch. Stardust's stride lengthened. Thunder Mountain, straining and foaming with sweat, felt the pseudo-horse surge alongside. He put on another burst of speed. But he was no match for Gadget's fingers on the dial. Stardust came neck and neck with Thunder Mountain.

In a close finish there was still no argument. Stardust had won!

Cliff turned unhappily to Hank. "I thought you said that Thunder Mountain could run," he said. "Oh well, easy come, easy go. Mr. O'Dowd," he added with a bow, "the money is yours, sir. And it is a pleasure to lose to such a gallant gentleman."

Gadget stood looking at the fluttering green money. His conscience was hurting him.

"Mr. Neary," he said, "perhaps I ought to tell you that that horse of mine—"

"No, no," said Cliff, "a race is a race." He was looking at the mounts as they came up. They were blowing and whistling from their run. "Say now, that's mighty peculiar. That Stardust of yours doesn't even seem to be winded."

Gadget's heel came down on the control box. And Stardust really began to blow.

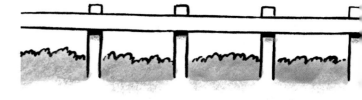

"No, he really isn't, I mean she really isn't," said Gadget. "In fact, I dare say, she could probably run another race if she had to."

Cliff looked up alertly. He glanced at the twelve bills and then at O'Dowd. "You don't mean to tell me that you'd be willing to risk another slight run for the money?"

"Well now," said Gadget reluctantly, "I think I probably owe it to you, Mr. Neary. Just the same—"

"Well, say no more," said Cliff. "Hank, bring up Sassy Lassie and we'll spin her around again. That is, of course, Mr. O'Dowd, if you have no objections?" If a man wanted to run a tired horse, who was Cliff Neary to refuse the money.

Gadget didn't, and the horses were soon lined into position. Sassy Lassie turned out to be a high-strung filly that the perspiring Pat found hard to manage. She tried to climb the rail, then the starting gate and finally consented to stay in position. Twenty-four thousand dollars, twelve of it in the form of a check on Cliff's bank, were now secured by the rock.

"We can't wait forever," said Cliff, afraid Stardust would get rested, "let 'em go."

The pistol banged, the gate lifted, and horse and reasonable-copy-thereof rocketed out into the track. Angus was standing high up, madly chewing Brown's Mule tobacco and wondering about the strength of the various pins and cogs.[*] He was wishing that he had foreseen this turn of affairs when he was at his forge.

Gadget, having secretly tuned Stardust's radar eyes to a set distance off the rail, looked up to Angus anxiously for a signal. Gadget's conscience was hurting him. He liked Cliff because Cliff was a swell guy. "But when he finds out what the cause is he'll laugh about it," Gadget apologized to himself. Many times before he had vowed that he would pay the studio and his victims back once the fact had been accomplished and man had made a voyage to the moon. His conscience thus made easier, he was willing to forget it and enjoy the horse race.

Angus was making wild motions and Gadget upped the speed notch, only to find out that Angus's arm signals became wilder. Accordingly, Gadget slowly backed it down again. An action which resulted in the Scot's relaxation.

The filly and Stardust came scrambling into the stretch, pounding forward, straining every muscle and bolt. Stardust was about eight lengths in the lead. Gadget understood his mechanic's earlier concern. Evidently the pseudo-horse had been traveling like a jet around the first turn. Gadget backed off the control dial even further and let Sassy Lassie catch up. They finished in a cloud of dust and hurrahs, out of which the fact appeared that Sassy Lassie had been whipped by half a length.

After a little, Pat and Tony came back. The jockey was blowing and round-eyed.

"Mr. Neary," said Pat, "that there Stardust run away from me at the start like an airplane. I didn't think I'd ever catch up."

"It's all right, Pat," said Cliff. "Somedays you can't ever see the back of your neck. Mr. O'Dowd, that's some horse you've got there. I wish there was a little more light, I'd like to look at her teeth."

"Oh, her teeth are just fine, fine," said Gadget.

"I'm serious," said Cliff. "Now probably you've got a lot of things to do besides monkey with a hobby like racehorses. Personally, it's not very profitable. And if you are just starting out you ought to take the advice of the old master and give it up at the beginning, while you are still on the winning end. There, you're twenty-four thousand dollars richer—"

"Eighteen," said Gadget. "I've got no objection to horse racing, Mr. Neary. There are just some people who can make money out of it and some people can't. Didn't you say that you had another horse around here?"

"Well, fan my brow," said Cliff. "Don't tell me that that filly of yours can run again?"

"It's like this," said Gadget, "I've raised her up from a . . . colt. She wouldn't be nothing but skin and bones if it weren't for me. And she knows it. She appreciates a good trainer when she has one. She'd be happy to run another race. Of course, I'll admit it's kind of dark—"

"See here, now," said Cliff, "if you think you can do it without exhausting her, I've got Old

Hundred over here. He's one of the fastest horses I ever had in my stables. If you don't mind taking another check?"

There was a sliver of the moon showing in the west. Gadget cocked one eye at it and then looked at Cliff. "Mr. Neary, that check is good enough for me."

Old Hundred came up and went down. And when the dust had settled, Cliff stood with his hands in the pockets of his leather jacket, the brim of his hat pulled down, and his shoulders hunched with chill.

"I'm sorry, Mr. Neary," said Pat, climbing down from Old Hundred. "When we got into the stretch I just plain couldn't even see that filly's tail. She was that far ahead. Maybe I just ain't much of a rider, Mr. Neary."

"Oh, say not so," said Cliff, putting his arm around Pat's shoulders. "You're just up against a wonder horse, that's all." He snapped his fingers, whistled, and looked at Gadget. "That's three times I've been beaten, Mr. O'Dowd. You wouldn't consider selling that horse, would you?"

With Angus and Tony looking on and gaping, O'Dowd gazed first at his toes, then at the moon, and then at Mr. Neary. Gadget knew his danger here. If he didn't go along with this sale, Cliff, horse-hungry, would become more and more insistent, finally discovering the extremely mechanical identity of Stardust—a discovery which would lead to argument.

"Well, I might entertain an option," said Gadget, "on one condition."

"Well, now, a little old thing like a condition," said Cliff, "shouldn't stand between a couple of good horse traders."

"The condition is that she won't ever be used for breeding purposes."

"I think that could be arranged," said Cliff. He looked kind of sly and disinterested. "Would . . . er . . . fifty thousand dollars make the deal

attractive? Say, ten thousand now as a down payment and forty thousand dollars tomorrow?"

"Oh, I can't deliver her right away," said Gadget. "She's on a special diet and I wouldn't dare take her off of it. You'd be surprised how that diet affects her. I have been making some scientific observations on her, too. And they won't be complete till Thursday morning."

Angus and Tony looked on in amazement. They had never got used to the glib and convincing way Gadget had with him when the necessity demanded it.

"Why Thursday morning?" said Cliff.

"Well, I've got to observe the final effects of this diet. And then you can have her."

"You'll give me the diet, too?"

"You bet I will," said Gadget.

Cliff finished writing out his check and gave Gadget his hand. "It's a deal, my boy. My trainer will be up at your place Thursday morning to pick up the filly. Come along, Hank, let's get out of this place while we still have enough money left to pay Uncle Sam his income tax. Goodbye, Mr. Marconio and Mr. McBane. Come on, Pat, you'll be riding winners yet."

Gadget stood looking after them as they left.

Angus grabbed his arm. "Och, laddie, how terrible it will be, the sight of you behind bars. Not only are you sellin' him somethin' that ain't a horse, but it's the property of United Pictures. Crime does not pay, me boy."

"Not very well, anyway," said Gadget thinking of Miss Franklin. "But cheer up. We have till Thursday morning to think up the rest of the idea."

"You mean you don't know?" said Tony.

"No, not yet," said Gadget.

"What a noive,"* said Tony, "what a noive! Let's load up and get out of here before you have any more of these half-thought-up ideas."

"Remind me when we get home to put the entry in my book: 'Eighteen thousand dollars to be paid back with interest to Mr. Cliff Neary.' He was just too nice about it. I haven't got the heart to take the money without putting it in my book to be paid off. Even if we did win it fair and square. After all, he asked us to race, we didn't ask him," Gadget said.

"What about the down payment?" Tony asked.

"Don't worry, we'll figure out something." Gadget seemed rather cheered now that he had decided to put Cliff's name in the book as one of those to be repaid when the trip was finally made. He fingered the checks and even whistled a little on the way home.

The Automagic Horse Becomes a Movie Star

Stardust having successfully broken down six doors without having sustained any injury, left the western set north of San Fernando in a shocking state of disrepair and on Wednesday the shooting of the picture started on schedule.

At seven o'clock in the morning everybody bundled up and went on out to the location at Gray's Ranch. Amongst the usual fooling around between the cameramen and the assistant directors, Gadget looked over the scene of action.

A big flimsy barn had been built. The roof beam was sawed half through and when the building burned, that roof would come down, but quick. Wires and pulleys would assist the cave-in of the roof and mounds of hay containing flares were piled all about. The property man was giving the hay a final sloshing with a smoke-making solution. There had to be a lot of smoke.

The stunt man went over the place to make sure there was nothing to trip over. He was a devil-may-care young man to all appearances. But in common with all good stunt men, the largest part of his dare-devilry consisted of the great care with which he planned the staging of his scenes. He bore[*] several scars and had a slight limp, all of which came from some director's miscalculation in regard to falling off cliffs or leaping through plate-glass windows.

The stunt man spent a few moments with Gadget going over the details of the shot.

Veronica Morris and Peter Butler were there eating a late breakfast in the shade of Butler's dressing-room trailer. Marty Fitzgibbons was entertaining them with an English music-hall story.

"Hello, Gadget," Mr. Butler called out. "That's Gadget O'Dowd over there," he told Miss Morris.

"Where? Oh, hello, Mr. O'Dowd. I hope you fixed it so that poor stunt man won't get hurt. I'd feel pretty dreadful if anything happened to him for my sake."

"He'll make it all right," said Gadget, accepting the leg of chicken that Mr. Butler's valet[*] handed him.

"Let's see it," said Mr. Butler, interested and getting up.

"Now, now, folks," said the director. "There's no hurry about this. Morning, Miss Morris. I'll have a cup of that coffee if you don't mind. Well, I see that you got the horse here all right, Gadget."

"I want to see that thing in action," said Mr. Butler. "I almost died laughing over that mechanical monkey Gadget built for the last Tarzan picture."

"Oh, I remember that," said Miss Morris. "He was certainly a wonderful 'animal.' Where is it now, Mr. O'Dowd? I don't suppose you could be persuaded to part with it?"

"The last I saw of it," said Gadget, "it was jumping up and down on the lead actor's front lawn. When the accountancy department gets through with me I suppose it will be lying on the scrap-metal heap in some local junk yard."

A cameraman came up with an assistant director. "We got three cameras on it, sir."

"Well, make sure you get it the first time," said the director. "That barn will only burn once."

Gadget put down the chicken bone. "I suppose that's my cue," he said.

"I've got to see this," said Mr. Butler. He picked up his "bad man's hat" and followed O'Dowd over toward the horse trailer. Angus was ready with the control box. And Tony let down the back gate. Stardust stopped being immobile* and began to champ* and whinny. She backed down the ramp, turned, pricked up her ears and, at Gadget's tip-off wink to Angus, Stardust came nuzzling up to Veronica Morris for a piece of sugar.

"Why, it's a real horse," said Veronica.

"Not if you put your ear to it," said Gadget.

"Why, that's Stardust," said Mr. Butler, "that won the sweepstakes."

The director took one look and turned to the script girl. They put their heads together for a moment and the director came up. "It won't do," he said. "Two scenes further along, that we've already shot, have a chestnut without any forehead markings."

"Sorry," said Gadget. "They didn't give me a script. Angus, hand that box of paint down here."

In a very short space of time, water color had remedied the situation handsomely. And the script girl was satisfied. The property man came over and saddled Stardust with the proper riding equipment. The stunt man gave his mount wide-eyed admiration.

"Mind if I try a couple of tests on it?" he said. He mounted up. Gadget made the horse prance, dance, and strike with its front feet. Finally he put Stardust into a dashing run.

"Well, for once," said the cameraman, "we won't have to speed the film up on that one. That hunk of junk can really get out of here."

The director gave the order for "Places!" The sound man took his tests. The front doors to the barn were securely barred on the stunt man. Gadget took up his position just off scene, where he could look

through a window into the barn, see the front door and the road which went off along the side of the corral. He had his control box all adjusted and tuned.

"Camera!" said the director. "Action!" An expert archer sent a blazing arrow across the scene into an explosives-loaded hay pile at the front of the barn. A second firebrand* followed it, sticking in the side wall. A third thunked solidly into the shingles and in a moment the dry explosive-laden material flared and yellow fire curled greedily across the structure. More hay piles caught. A second stunt man ran forward. He was dressed in historical costume. He pitched a torch in through the barn window.

The flames were beginning to crackle and roar. Gadget waited until the entire front of the building was blazing. Then, with an urgent wave from the assistant director, he set Stardust in motion. The roof was already beginning to sway. The temperature in the barn must have mounted to about a hundred and thirty degrees. Stardust began to plunge and rear.

Then it dashed forward, flung up its hoofs, and brought them down solidly against the doors.

Outside, on signals, two soldiers came up to lower muskets* at the entrance. The doors caved. The assistant director's men gave a yank and the roof started down.

Out came Stardust! Narrowly missed by two blazing beams, nearly swallowed in clouds of white smoke and billows of yellow fire! The stunt man dressed in lady's riding clothes was leaning on the neck and holding on in earnest. Stardust plunged, pretended to rear at

the two extras, who now blazed away with their two muskets, and fled off down the road at a fast run! Arrows and crossbow bolts thunked in her wake. She vanished far up the lane. The director called "Break!"

Next followed three shots, done on another set, of the now somewhat singed Stardust plunging and rearing in a mock interior. She had to break down a burning door in here, too. At eleven o'clock the work was finished. And, mounted on a real horse, Veronica Morris was ready to follow through with the closeups. Mr. Butler was due to "perish" tomorrow. So today he could look on.

Gadget having lunched with the director and chief cameraman, receiving praise all around for his remarkable horse, was now free to return to his laboratory and do what he considered more important work.

As Gadget and Tony were backing Stardust up to the horse trailer they had one slight encounter with the S.P.C.A. representative who wanted to examine the "injuries sustained by the horse in that last scene." In the end, the man, who turned out to be quite a nice fellow after all, was their most appreciative audience. He just couldn't get over it. They let him examine a couple of the bolts down the throat, and unscrew a couple of teeth. "You are a genius, my boy," he said. "You are a genius. You should have proper recognition. Why, there are museums all over the country—"

"Oh no," Gadget said hurriedly, "I could never do it again. It was just a fluke."

They finally escaped from the terrible prospect of the very unprofitable "proper recognition." "That was a narrow one," said Gadget as the man walked away. "If we ever got 'recognition' we wouldn't make enough to fly to Canada, much less the moon."

They loaded the scorched Stardust into the trailer and wheeled on home.

Miss Franklin was waiting for them. She had, gripped in her hand, a green slip of paper which she had obviously been holding half of the morning in anticipation of their return. Gadget took one look at it and knew what it was: the twenty-five-hundred-and-twenty-dollar kickback from the racing museum, twenty-eight hundred dollars minus ten percent.

"Now don't tell me this is a personal debt," said Miss Franklin in a silky voice. "The boy told me that he was to give it only to Gadget O'Dowd."

"Then how did you get it?" said Gadget.

Tony looked mournfully at a torn up flower bed. "Boss, she can wrastle, too."

"That skin the racing museum gave your mechanic can go right back to them. It will cost me a whole lot less than twenty-eight hundred dollars to have it restuffed. It looks to me, Mr. O'Dowd, like you didn't need any such budget. This makes you exactly two thousand and five hundred and twenty dollars under your estimate."

Gadget looked at her and sighed deeply. He went into his own office and slammed the door.

Gadget and His Friends Win the Day

The following morning bright and early Cliff's trainer, Hank, drove up with a horse trailer which made the rental job look like something from a junk yard. His men opened the door of this glittering creation invitingly. Hank went into the office to find Mr. O'Dowd. Fortunately, Miss Franklin considered her office hours to be from nine to five. Movie people are ordinarily up long before that.

"Well, well," said Hank, "here I am."

"Well, well," said Gadget, "I see you are."

"Shall we load the horse aboard now?"

"Well, you see," said Gadget, "I've been thinking this thing over rather carefully and I've decided—"

"You're not going to back out on the deal now?" said Hank.

"Well," said Gadget, "I was thinking—"

"Mr. O'Dowd," said Hank, "you look to me like a man of your word. You wouldn't go back on Mr. Neary, would you? He could do you a lot of good."

"That isn't all he could do to him," said Angus under his breath.

Gadget was thinking fast. If he confessed this sin he would certainly have to refund Cliff's losses. But if he didn't, then he would have to give Cliff the horse. Due to his disturbed state of mind because of the twenty-five-hundred-and-twenty-dollar hole in the budget he had not come up with the brilliant idea of which he had thought himself capable.

"Where is the horse?" said Hank suspiciously. "She's all right, isn't she?"

Gadget was about to report the theft of Stardust when one of the men spotted her in the bar. "Funny place to keep a horse," said Hank.

"I hope she doesn't drink! Well, shall we load up?"

"She looks kind of singed," said one of the men. "What happened?"

"Nothing serious," said Gadget. "Nothing serious at all."

"Funny look about that horse," said the other man.

"Well, she's just a little bit off her feed today. All that running didn't help her any. Tony, we are being very thoughtless in our hospitality. Take these gentlemen inside and give them something to eat or drink."

"I got a fresh cup of coffee if you want some," Tony said.

"You go ahead too, Hank. I'll put her in the trailer," Gadget said.

Tony hustled them inside, and Gadget loaded Stardust on board the super-deluxe horse trailer. When they came out again, Hank saw Stardust's ears above the trailer side, handed Gadget the check from Mr. Neary and they agreed to sign all the necessary papers on Saturday morning. Hands were shaken all around and soon the yard was deserted.

Ten seconds later Miss Franklin drove on the scene.

"What was that horse trailer?" she demanded.

The smile which Gadget had worn at the departure now vanished. "Well, you see, that Stardust—"

"You mean you've let somebody else have a piece of property belonging to United Pictures? You must realize that there is a lot of valuable equipment in there that can be salvaged," said Miss Franklin primly. "You've already exceeded your—"

"D'ye mean to say that we've got to go to all the toil of taking that horse apart?" said Angus, coming late to work.

"I mean just that," said Miss Franklin. "We'll restore that hide to the museum and put all the various parts on the inventory." She went into her office and could be heard arranging things for her day.

Gadget looked at Angus. "Bring the control box out," he said.

Angus was in no mood to be lightly ordered about, but he went. "Dismantlin' a horse!" he was snorting. "Filing parts! Inventory! What the movie business isna comin' to would— What in the saintly name has happened to this control box?" He came back out, his basic anger building. "Musther O'Dowd! Some rat has unsoldered—!"

"Give it here," said Gadget hastily. "I was in a hurry. I didn't know when they'd look at me. Give me that box!"

Miss Franklin, curious as to what was going on out in the courtyard, came out of her office, aggressive as an overdue bill. "What are you doing?" she demanded. "When the business office learns—"

Suddenly a roaring whine resounded in the sky. Looking up, a terrified Miss Franklin beheld a horse! It had been rising ever since the trailer had begun to move, having gone straight up, and now it had a very, very long way to come down.

Miss Franklin screamed! Stardust was falling faster now, falling with the gathering speed of a bomb, falling so fast that the air was split and scorched.

Down came Stardust from its suspended station. Down came Stardust getting bigger and bigger, louder and louder. Down came Stardust with a crash!

Dust shot away! Hoofs and hide contracted, seemed buried in the earth and then bounced with a geyser of wheels, cogs, tubes and useless condensers. Up went the electronic shower, down came distended* rods and shattered bric-a-brac, mingled with spattering, twisted pieces of torn hide.

Stillness came. A radar eye rolled pathetically* to Gadget's feet and lay there, teetering, looking at him accusatively. The dust settled slowly, quietly, and much of it upon a cowering* Miss Franklin whose shattered nerves were almost as damaged as the late and unlamented automagic horse.

"Gravity repulsor," said Gadget O'Dowd. "Installed it at the last minute in a streak of proud genius. Works fine, doesn't it, Angus?" He looked kindly at Miss Franklin. "Gravity repulsor, installed to conduct a scientific experiment in the interests of the future safety of stunt men. Solder seems to have broken so that I couldn't slow it down."

73

"What . . . what happened?" said Miss Franklin.

"Why," said Gadget, "in the interests of picture research, we installed a gravity repulsor which lifted Stardust out of the trailer and placed her back here where she belongs. And I think you will find that this experiment cost exactly twenty-five hundred and twenty dollars to conduct, including the cost of the gravity repulsor unit, of course." He looked brightly at the scattered remains which were strewn widely across the flower beds.

Miss Franklin gulped, looked at Gadget with baffled but dawning respect and then took her tired way into her office.

"Loddie,"* said Angus, "'tis a great project on which we're embarked. But I'm thinkin' if ye keep this up ye'll find it necessary to go to the moon—aye, and a divil* of a lot farther before we're done."

"Boss," said the worshipful Tony, "that sure was a bang-up solution to dat problem!"

Gadget reached into his jacket pocket and brought out the purchase checks which Mr. Neary had given him for the sale of Stardust. He handed them to Tony. "This hurts me more than I can say, but one must be honest after all. Take them over to Mr. Neary and tell him how sorry we are that his new horse ran away. Tell him it was a bad habit she had anyway."

"Give him back fifty thousand dollars?" gaped Tony.

"My boy," said Gadget, "you have evidently forgotten how much money we made off him on the bets. My conscience," he added, with a bright, self-denying smile, "wouldn't permit me to keep his checks for a horse he never owned."

"Your conscience," said Tony, with disgust, "is the most expensive thing we got!" He pulled on his gloves, took the money and drove away.

In the dark of night another mile of tunnel to a "gamma room" was started into the Hollywood Hills. And enough metal for a spaceship's bow was smuggled, the very next day, straight under the watchful nose of Miss Franklin.

Gadget and Angus and Tony were that much closer to the moon. "I hope humanity appreciates the trouble we've gone to for it," said Gadget. But there was so much noise around the busy forge that Angus and Tony didn't even hear him.

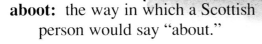

Glossary

aboot: the way in which a Scottish person would say "about."

ain: the way in which a Scottish person would say "own."

alpha pile: a device for starting and maintaining a series of actions to produce atomic energy.

arrested: stopped in motion.

balk: to stop and refuse to move or act.

behind the wire: refers to being behind the starting line in a horse race.

bit player: one who plays small parts in movies.

blank cartridge pistol: refers to a pistol that has no bullet in it, but still makes a loud noise when fired; sometimes used to start a race with its sound.

boded: gave a sign of a future event.

Bogart, Humphrey: famous movie star from the 1930s, 1940s and 1950s known early in his screen career for playing gangster roles.

bookie: a person who makes a business of accepting bets on horse races.

booster: a device that increases the amount of electricity flowing through a wire.

bore: had or showed a certain mark.

bric-a-brac: odds and ends of any sort.

budgeteering: comes from "budget," the plan for how money will be spent. Budgeteering is the act of preparing or using a budget.

careen: to lean or roll from side to side while moving fast.

cathode-ray tube: a display screen, like that of a television, on which beams of energy are projected to produce a picture.

champ: to show impatience; be restless.

clip: a high rate of speed.

cog: a row of teeth, on the edge of a wheel, which fits between the teeth on another wheel so when one turns it can turn the other.

condenser: a device used for storing electricity.

corn: something which is repeated so often people are tired of hearing it.

cowering: shaking with fear.

crack a bank: rob a bank.

cue: any signal, hint or suggestion.

cuffed: hit with the open hand; slapped.

czar: an absolute, all-powerful ruler.

deadlock: a complete standstill or lack of progress.

dean: the senior or leading member of a group.

didna: the way in which a Scottish person would say "didn't."

dinna: the way in which a Scottish person would say "doesn't."

distended: expanded or stretched.

divil: the way in which a Scottish person would say "devil."

don: to put on, as one's hat or coat.

draw: to earn (weekly pay, for example).

duplicated: when there are two or more items that are the same, they are "duplicated."

electrodes: two points electricity travels between. Electricity flows out of one point, across a distance (through the air), and into the other point.

English exercise pad: a small saddle used by a rider when exercising a horse.

firebrand: a piece of burning wood.

forge: furnace for heating metal to be hammered into shape.

futile: hopeless.

gallant: brave and good; courageous.

gamma ray: a powerful type of energy that is dangerous in high amounts and can penetrate solid materials like lead and steel. "Gamma" is a letter of the Greek alphabet chosen as the name for this kind of ray.

gnaw: to bite and wear away bit by bit with the teeth.

gravity repulsor: a device used to push something away from the ground up into the air. To repulse is to push away from.

groom: a person whose work is taking care of horses.

grubbing: working hard for.

harbor: to hide.

highroad: a simple, direct or sure path.

immobile: not moving or changing.

isna: the way in which a Scottish person would say "is not."

jaunt: a trip or journey, especially one taken for pleasure.

keerful: the way in which a Scottish person would say "careful."

like a ton of bricks: with great speed and weight.

loddie: the way in which a Scottish person would say "laddie."

manganese: a grayish-white metal.

Man-of-War: a famous racing horse from the 1920s.

measly: worthless or skimpy.

mid-rear: rising up halfway on the hind legs.

musket: a gun with a long barrel used from the mid-1500s to early 1800s.

niche: a place or position (such as a job) that fits a person.

noive: the way in which a person from New York would say "nerve," which means boldness that is without shame or that shows disrespect.

onnatural: the way in which a Scottish person would say "unnatural."

occasioned: brought about.

onslaught: a fierce attack.

oot: the way in which a Scottish person would say "out."

option: the right to buy or sell something at a certain price within a certain time.

pathetically: causing or deserving pity.

prance: to rise up on the hind legs in a lively way, especially while moving along; said of a horse.

prime: the best period in the life of a person.

projected: planned (a course of action, for example).

pseudo: not real.

R.C.A.: (Radio Corporation of America) a large company that makes many kinds of electronic parts and equipment.

rally: to recover suddenly, from a setback or disadvantage.

rambling: (of a house or street or village, etc.) extending in various directions irregularly.

rearing: rising up on the hind legs.

relay: a type of switch used in an electric device to turn other devices on and off.

resound: to make a loud echoing sound.

retort: to answer back, especially in a sharp or clever way.

rub dis dame out: a gangster expression meaning "to kill this woman." ("Rub out" means to "kill"; "dis" is the word "this" said by a person from New York; "dame" is a slang term for "woman.")

saffron: a bright orange yellow.

sage: having wisdom gained from experience.

Santa Anita: a well-known racetrack in the Los Angeles area.

saunter: to walk about slowly, not in a hurry; stroll.

scurvy: a disease resulting from a lack of vitamin C.

sired: to be the male parent.

spittoon: a container to spit into.

spur: a pointed part or attachment sticking out of something. For example, an attachment to a building.

Stage: the whole working section of a theater, including the acting area, the backstage area, etc.

swine: a hated person or thing.

tam-o'-shanter: a Scottish cap with a round, flat top.

taxidermist: one who stuffs and mounts the skins of dead animals so that they look alive.

touts: people who provide information to gamblers about a horse race (such as which horse could win) for a fee.

transformer: a device that changes the amount of electricity flowing through a wire.

travail: very hard work.

trunk: a body, not including the head, arms and legs.

tube: an electric device that affects energy passing through it. Tubes are commonly used for electric signs.

twa: the way in which a Scottish person would say "two."

t'would: the way in which a Scottish person would say "it would."

United Nations: an international peace-seeking organization of about 150 countries.

valet: a man who works as a servant for another man.

verge: the edge, border.

volt: a unit for measuring the force of an electrical current.

"wall of light": the speed of light. "Breaking the wall of light" means to go faster than the speed of light.

Westinghouse: (Westinghouse Electric Corporation) a very large company that produces many kinds of electrical equipment.

what: (British expression) used to get agreement.

whin: the way in which a Scottish person would say "when."

whust: the way in which a Scottish person would say "My goodness."

whut: the way in which a Scottish person would say "what."

wi'out: the way in which a Scottish person would say "without."

woise: the way in which a person from New York would say "worse."

wul': the way in which a Scottish person would say "well."

L. Ron Hubbard

During a highly successful 56-year writing career, master storyteller L. Ron Hubbard wrote and published more than 260 tales of adventure, romance, mystery, suspense, science fiction, fantasy and the American West.

In the last 10 years alone, 34 of his books have been national bestsellers and more than 116 million of his fiction and non-fiction works have been sold in over 100 countries around the world.

Scott E. Sutton

Scott E. Sutton is a highly versatile illustrator and author who has successfully combined his talents in a growing number of colorful and informative books for children, including such popular series as, *The Family of Ree, The Kuekumber Kids* and *The Adventures of Dinosaur Dog*.